Pooh's **Heffalump** Movie

Walt Disney's The Many Adventures Of **WINNIE The POOH**

Disney Piglet's **BIG** Movie

Disney THE **Tigger** MOVIE

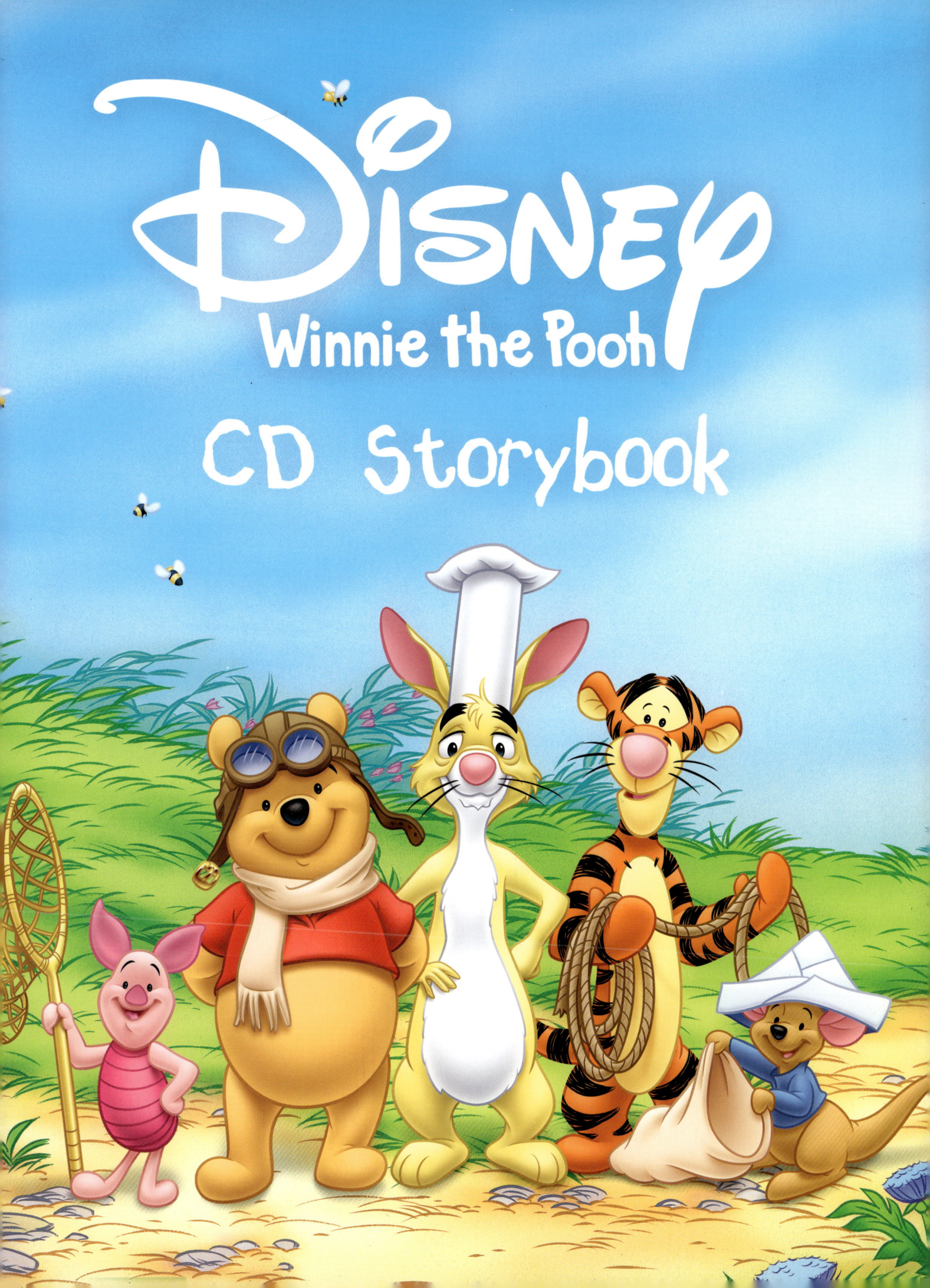

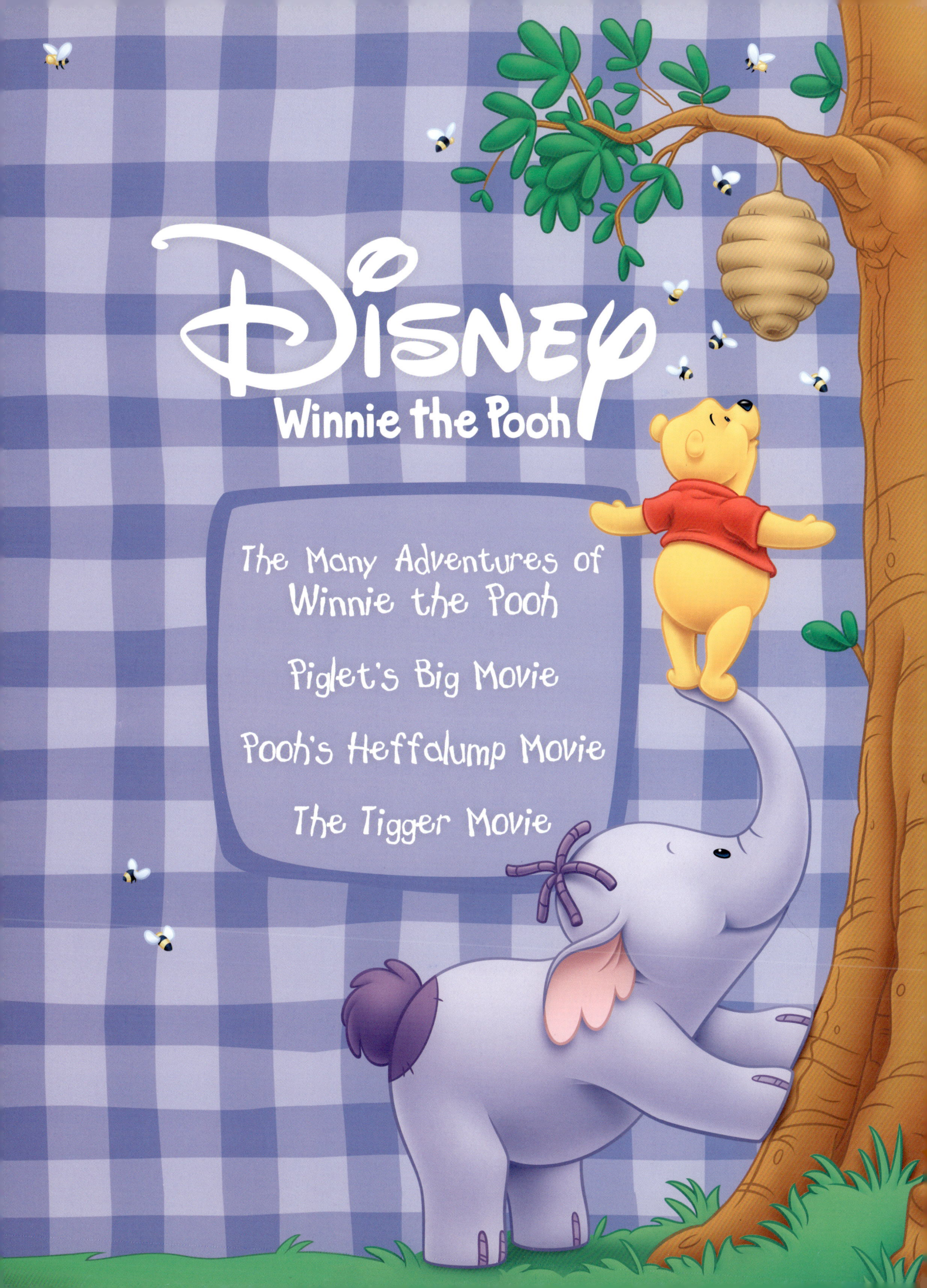

Hinkler Books Pty Ltd 2005
17-23 Redwood Drive
Dingley, VIC, 3172
www.hinklerbooks.com

Based on the 'Winnie the Pooh' works,
by A. A. Milne and E. H. Shepard

© Disney Enterprises, Inc.

Stories adapted by Karen Comer
Book design by Hinkler Design Studio

All Rights Reserved. Without limiting the rights under copyright above,
no part of this publication may be reproduced, stored in or introduced
into a retrieval system, or transmitted in any form or by any means
(electronic, mechanical, photocopying, recording or otherwise), without
the prior written permission of The Walt Disney Company.

ISBN 1 7412 1969 8

Printed and manuctured in China.

Contents

The Many Adventures of Winnie the Pooh 7

Piglet's Big Movie 37

Pooh's Heffalump Movie 67

The Tigger Movie 97

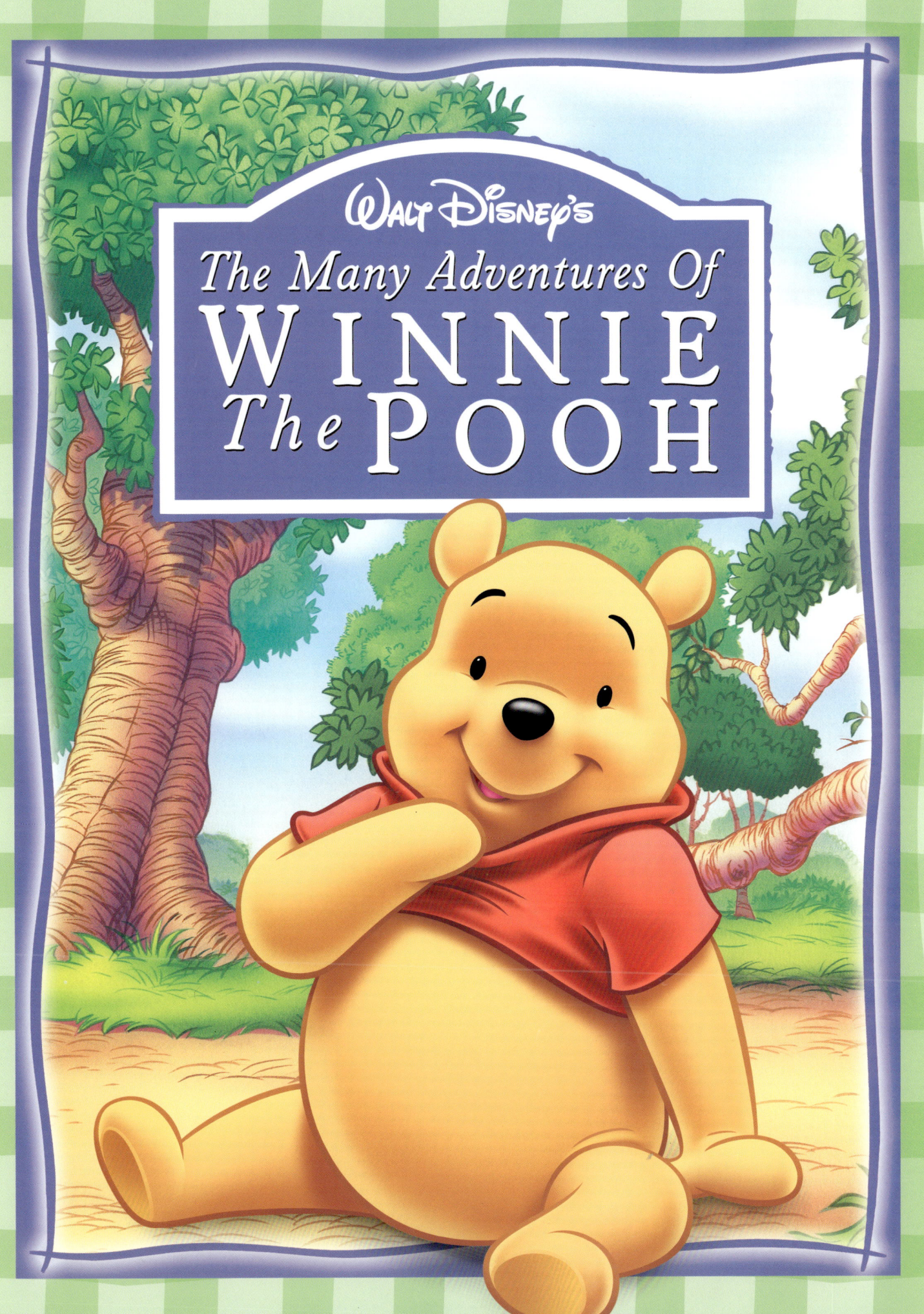

Winnie the Pooh, whose friends called him Pooh for short, lived in the Hundred-Acre Wood, where he had many unusual adventures.

One morning, Pooh heard his Pooh-coo clock chime, and he knew it was time for something. But being a bear of very little brain, when he thought, he thought very hard.

"Think, think, think . . ." Pooh said. "Oh, yes! Time for my stoutness exercises!"

So Pooh bent down and touched his toes in front of the mirror. And as soon as he did, he was hungry again!

Since Pooh had worked up an appetite, he reached inside his cupboard for some honey. Then he heard a buzzing noise.

"That buzzing noise means something . . . and the only reason for making a buzzing noise that I know of is because you're a . . . bee! And the only reason for being a bee is to make honey . . . and the only reason for making honey is . . . so I can eat it!" Pooh reasoned.

So Pooh followed the bee to a tree and began to climb it. He balanced on a branch and reached inside the tree hollow where the bees made honey. But the branch snapped, and Pooh fell down, down, down, into a gorse bush below.

Pooh crawled out of the bush, brushed himself off, and began to think. The first person he thought of who might be of help was Christopher Robin. So Pooh went off to find him.

Pooh soon found his friend Christopher Robin.

"I was thinking and wondering if you had such a thing as a balloon about you," Pooh said hopefully.

"What do you want a balloon for?" asked Christopher Robin.

"Honey!" whispered Pooh.

"But you don't get honey with a balloon!" Christopher Robin replied.

"I do!" Pooh said cheerfully. "I shall fly like a bee, up to the honey tree."

Christopher Robin was a bit doubtful that Pooh's plan would work.

What Christopher Robin didn't know was that Pooh had an idea to disguise himself. He went to a very muddy place and rolled and rolled until he was black all over. Then he went back to show Christopher Robin.

"Isn't this a clever disguise?" said Pooh, chuckling to himself, and he took the balloon from Christopher Robin.

"What are you suppose to be?" asked Christopher Robin, a little confused.

"I'm a little black rain cloud, of course," Pooh replied matter-of-factly.

"Silly old Bear," laughed Christopher Robin.

And so Christopher Robin gently let Pooh and the balloon up into the air. Pooh drifted over to the honey tree.

As Pooh came closer to the tree, the bees began to come out of their hive and buzzed around him angrily.

"Christopher Robin!" called Pooh. "I think the bees suspect something. I think it would help with the deception if you'd open your umbrella and say, 'Tut tut, it looks like rain.'"

Christopher Robin did as Pooh asked, but the bees started to sting Pooh.

They pushed Pooh away from the honey tree. He held on tightly to the balloon as the bees chased him to the ground. Pooh and Christopher Robin jumped into a puddle, and Christopher Robin held up his umbrella over them until the bees flew away.

Now Pooh was not the sort to give up easily. When he put his mind to honey, he stuck to it!

So Pooh went to visit his friend Rabbit.

"Pooh? Lunch? Not again!" cried Rabbit from inside his house, as he heard Pooh coming.

"Is anybody at home?" called Pooh.

"Nobody!" called back Rabbit.

Pooh thought to himself. "Somebody must be there, because somebody must have said 'Nobody.'"

Rabbit grudgingly let Pooh in and offered him lunch.

So Pooh ate and ate and ate. And ate and ate and ate, until there was no more honey.

But when it came time to leave, Pooh found himself stuck in Rabbit's front door.

"Oh bother!" said Pooh.

Rabbit tried to push him through, but it was no use. Rabbit went out his back door to find Christopher Robin.

Christopher Robin decided that the only thing to do was to wait for Pooh to become thin enough to fit through the door.

Christopher Robin, Kanga, Roo and the others looked after Pooh. They made sure he wasn't wet when it rained, and that he was warm enough. But they didn't give him anything to eat, no matter how much Pooh wanted it.

And then, eventually, when Pooh was just a little thinner, they were able to pull him out.

But Pooh went flying into the air. He landed in the honey tree, head first in the beehive.

"There he goes!" said Rabbit.

"Stuck again," noted Eeyore gloomily.

"Don't worry, Pooh, we'll get you out!" shouted Christopher Robin at the tree.

Pooh had his hands and mouth in the honey. "No hurry, take your time," he said as he slurped the honey.

Soon after, Pooh had another unusual adventure. He decided to visit his thoughtful spot on a blustery day. Since Pooh was a bear of very little brain, whenever he thought, he thought in the most thoughtful way he could think.

But he was interrupted from his thinking by a gopher. "If I were you, I'd think about getting out of here—it's Windsday . . ."

"It is?" replied Pooh. "Then I think I shall wish everyone a happy Windsday, and I shall begin with my dear friend, Piglet."

Now Piglet's house was in another part of the forest. It was a very grand house in the middle of a beech tree. And Piglet loved it very much.

Piglet was trying to sweep up the leaves blowing around his house when Pooh arrived. But the blustery wind blew Piglet right up into the air!

Pooh reached up and managed to grab Piglet's scarf. But it began to unravel.

Pooh held on tightly to the end of Piglet's scarf, which was now just a long piece of string. They rushed past Kanga and Roo, and Eeyore, and then Rabbit in his garden.

But the wind lifted Pooh into the air like Piglet. And both of them landed against Owl's window.

"Well, I say now!" cried Owl. "Someone has pasted Piglet on my window! And Pooh too!"

Owl opened his window, and Pooh and Piglet flew in. Owl offered them tea, while the wind blew and blew, rattling Owl's belongings and sending Pooh and Piglet flying from one end of the room to the other.

There was a great gust of wind, and Owl's house shuddered and fell to the ground. Fortunately, Pooh, Piglet and Owl were safe.

Christopher Robin came to survey the damage to Owl's house. "I don't think we will ever be able to fix it," he said.

"If you ask me," said Eeyore, "when a house looks like that, it's time to find another one. I'll find a new one for him."

The blustery day turned into a blustery night. At Pooh's house, it was a very anxious sort of night filled with anxious sorts of noises . . . and one of the noises was a sound that had never been heard before . . .

Now Pooh, being a bear of very little brain, decided to invite the new sound in.

"Hello out there," Pooh called, as he opened his front door and peered out. "Oh, I hope nobody answers."

But somebody did answer.

"Hello! I'm Tigger!" said Tigger, as he bounced inside. "Who are you?"

"I'm Pooh."

"What's a Pooh?" asked Tigger, as he bounced on top of him.

"You're sitting on one," replied Pooh, from underneath Tigger. "But what is a Tigger?"

"Hoo-hoo-hoo-hoo! Tiggers are the most wonderful things there are—they're bouncy and fun!" cried Tigger. "Well, I'd better be bouncing along now, chum. Cheerio!" And Tigger bounded away.

The very blustery night turned into a very rainy night. Piglet's house was flooded. He bobbed about on a wooden chair, trying to keep dry. In desperation, he wrote a note.

"Help! Piglet. Me." the note said. Piglet pushed it into a bottle and threw the bottle out his window.

Pooh was very concerned about his honeypots. He climbed up his tree with as many honeypots as he could carry. But as he put his head in a pot to check the honey level, he fell out of the tree, and landed in the water with his head in the pot.

Now Christopher Robin lived at the very top of the Wood. The water couldn't come up to his house, so that's where everyone gathered.

Roo made a very important discovery. "Look!" he shouted. "I've rescued a bottle."

"It's a message," said Christopher Robin, and he read Piglet's note. "Owl, you fly over to Piglet's house and tell him we'll make a rescue."

So Owl flew out over the flood and he soon spotted two tiny objects below him. One was Piglet caught in a whirlpool, and the other was Pooh trying to eat the last bit of honey from the honeypot.

Piglet and Pooh were heading dangerously close to a waterfall. They couldn't stop and went racing down with it. But they survived the waterfall, and floated along to Christopher Robin's house.

"Pooh, you rescued Piglet!" shouted Christopher Robin. "It was a very brave thing to do. You are a hero. And as soon as the flood is over, I shall give you a hero party."

At Pooh's hero party, Christopher Robin began to make a speech. "Attention, everybody. Now this party is a hero party because of what someone did . . . and this someone is . . ."

But Eeyore interrupted him. "I found it," he said. "House for Owl."

Everyone followed Eeyore to see Owl's new house.

"This is it—Owl's new house," said Eeyore who had unknowingly led them to Piglet's house.

Piglet gulped. "Oh, dear me." The others gasped.

Piglet said bravely, "This house does belong to our very good friend, Owl."

Rabbit asked, "But Piglet, where will you live?"

"Well, I guess I shall live . . ." Piglet stuttered.

"With me," said Pooh. "Christopher Robin, can you make a one hero party into a two hero party?"

And so Pooh was a hero for saving Piglet, and Piglet was a hero for giving Owl his grand home in the beech tree.

On a sunny morning, Pooh, who was a bear of very little brain, sat not thinking of anything in particular. All of a sudden, along came Tigger, who had a habit of bouncing in on his friends when they least expected him.

"Hello, Pooh!" Tigger greeted him. "I'm Tigger!"

Pooh chuckled. "Yes, I know. You've bounced me before."

"Well, I gotta go now. I got a lot of bouncing to do." And with that, Tigger left Pooh.

Tigger bounced into Rabbit, who was working in his vegetable garden, knocking him over and sending the vegetables flying.

"My beautiful garden!" cried Rabbit. "It's ruined!" Rabbit surveyed his damaged garden. "Oh, Tigger, why don't you ever stop bouncing?"

"Why, that's what Tiggers do best!" said Tigger, and he bounced away.

Rabbit called a protest meeting to stop Tigger from bouncing.

"It is time we taught him a lesson! No matter how much we like him, you can't deny it, he just bounces too much!" Rabbit said firmly.

Piglet thought. "Perhaps if we could think of a way of unbouncing Tigger . . ."

"I've got a splendid idea," Rabbit said. "We'll take Tigger for a long explore, someplace where he's never been, and lose him there!"

"Lose him?" asked Pooh in surprise.

"Oh, we'll find him again next morning, and mark my words, he'll be a different Tigger altogether," Rabbit said. "It'll take the bounces out of him."

So it was agreed, that they would start the next morning, which incidentally turned cold and misty. As they walked along, the mist kept getting thicker and thicker, and Tigger kept disappearing and appearing again.

But when Tigger had disappeared once more, Rabbit ushered Pooh and Piglet into a hollow log, where they hid from Tigger.

"Halloo!" shouted Tigger. "Where are you?"

"Shh," whispered Rabbit.

"I am shushed," Pooh whispered back.

When Tigger realized he couldn't find his friends, he went to look for them.

Rabbit, Pooh, and Piglet tried to find their way home in the mist, but they kept arriving back at the Sandy Pit.

"Hmm, it's a funny thing how everything looks the same in the mist," said Rabbit anxiously.

"Well, we keep looking for home, but we keep finding this pit, so I thought if we looked for this pit, we might find home," Pooh reasoned.

Rabbit sniffed. "I don't see much sense in that. If I walked away from this pit, and then walked back to it, of course I should find it. I'll prove it to you, wait here." So Rabbit left.

Pooh and Piglet waited and waited in the Sandy Pit, but Rabbit didn't return. And Pooh started thinking of his honeypots at home. So Pooh and Piglet set off for home, with Pooh following the call of his honeypots.

As the mist became thinner, and Piglet knew this part of the Wood, Tigger found them. Now, it seemed Rabbit was the only one missing, so Tigger decided to look for him.

Rabbit was still wandering around in the mist. By now he was lost and bewildered and terrified of all the forest noises, which sounded deafening in the mist.

"Help!" he called out.

"Hello, Rabbit!" said Tigger, bouncing up to him.

"Tigger? But you're supposed to be lost!" Rabbit said.

"Oh, Tiggers never get lost!" he replied. "Let's go home. Hang on!" Rabbit held onto Tigger's tail, while Tigger bounced him home.

The first snowfall had covered the Hundred-Acre Wood. Tigger arrived at Kanga and Roo's place, ready to play with Roo.

"Do Tiggers like to climb trees?" Roo asked, as they bounced through the forest.

"That's what Tiggers do best! Only Tiggers don't climb trees. They bounce them!" Tigger said.

And they bounced high up into a tall tree.

"Some bouncing, huh?" said Tigger. "Yeow! Say, how did this tree get so high?"

"What's the matter, Tigger?" asked Roo.

"I was just getting seasick from seeing too much," said Tigger, looking a little scared.

Pooh and Piglet found them. "Hello, Roo," said Pooh. "What are you and Tigger doing up there?"

"I'm alright," said Roo, "but Tigger's stuck."

Well, it wasn't long before word got back to Christopher Robin and the others that Tigger was in trouble.

"He can't bounce anybody up there," said Rabbit in satisfaction, looking up at Tigger in the tree.

But Christopher Robin took off his coat, and everyone held a corner of it. Roo jumped into the coat. "Gee, that was fun," he cried.

"You're next, Tigger," called Christopher Robin. "Jump!"

"Tiggers don't jump—they bounce," explained Tigger, looking down nervously.

"Then bounce down," said Pooh.

"Well, we'll just have to leave him up there forever," Rabbit said happily.

"Forever?" said Tigger. "Oh, if I ever get out of this I promise never to bounce again—never!"

So Tigger moved slowly along his branch, and nobody was quite sure whether he jumped or bounced or fell but somehow he ended up on the ground.

"Oh, I'm so happy, I feel like bouncing!" said Tigger, glad to be on the ground again.

"You promised!" warned Rabbit.

"You mean I can't ever bounce again?" Tigger asked miserably.

"Never!" declared Rabbit.

Tigger walked away sadly.

"Christopher Robin," said Roo. "I like the old bouncy Tigger best."

"So do I," agreed Christopher Robin. The others nodded.

"Rabbit?" said Kanga firmly.

"Oh, alright. I guess I like the old Tigger better too," Rabbit grudgingly agreed.

Tigger was back in an instant. "You mean I can have my bounce back?" he asked happily. And he started to bounce, and the others joined in too.

Piglet was working on his scrapbook, a beautiful collection of drawings of the many adventures he and his friends had had in the Hundred-Acre Wood.

As he looked out his window, Piglet thought his friends must be having another amazing adventure right then. He was surprised to see Pooh, Tigger, Eeyore and Rabbit parading by, dressed in unusual costumes. Piglet was curious. He put his scrapbook aside and went out to find them.

They were gathered in a little clearing, preparing for something, with a beehive made of paper, a megaphone, a violin and their costumes.

Pooh explained their big plan to Piglet. "First, Rabbit will lure the bees with beautiful music. Then Eeyore tempts the bees into their new hive. Then Tigger holds up the hive for the bees to see. And then comes the best part, we get honey from their old hive."

"Can I help you with your big plan?" asked Piglet.

"Oh, thank you, Piglet. But, um, perhaps another time," Pooh replied.

"When we have a bit smaller of a plan," added Tigger. "Or, when you're a bit bigger of a Piglet."

"I'm sorry, Piglet. But I'm afraid this is a very big plan," Rabbit said.

But the bees couldn't wait for the big plan. Tired of listening to Rabbit's music, they swarmed out of their hive, headed for Rabbit, and broke his violin into pieces.

Then the bees flew angrily towards Eeyore with his megaphone. Only Piglet noticed. He raced over to the megaphone, knocking it off its stand, moments before the bees would have flown into Eeyore's mouth.

But the bees descended on Piglet. He just managed to turn the megaphone as the bees flew through it, diverting the bees into the paper bee hive.

Piglet peeked into the hive and saw the angry bees. He quickly pasted a bit of paper across the opening to stop the bees from flying out.

Up in the tree, Rabbit turned the real hive upside down, and the honey poured out, all over Tigger and Pooh, instead of into Pooh's honeypot.

"We're geniuses!" shouted Tigger.

"Our plan worked perfectly," nodded Rabbit in satisfaction.

"Congratulations to us all!" said Pooh, and he put a sticky paw around Eeyore, Rabbit and Tigger.

No one had noticed Piglet's bravery.

"Oh, Piglet, I'm sorry that you couldn't be part of our big plan," said Rabbit.

"Oh, but . . . I thought that I . . ." stammered Piglet.

But the others continued to celebrate their success, without including Piglet. He walked away sadly.

Pooh was still happily eating honey, and his friends were still talking about their wonderful big plan, when they heard a buzzing noise.

"Did you hear something? I'm afraid I've got some honey in my ears," said Pooh.

Just then, the bees broke out of the paper hive. Pooh, Tigger, Eeyore and Rabbit froze in fear. Then they ran as fast as they could, with the bees chasing behind them.

The friends spotted Piglet's house, and ran towards it, slamming the door shut on the angry bees.

Piglet wandered through the Wood, upset because his friends didn't need him.

"It'd sure be nice if my friends needed me," Piglet thought. "I may be small, but in the biggest, helpfullest way!"

He went back to the clearing to find them, but there was no one there, not even the bees. Piglet realized what had happened—the bees must have chased his friends. He decided to go after them in case they needed help.

"Is everyone alright?" asked Rabbit. "Tigger's here. Eeyore's here. Pooh is here. I'm here. Hmm, who am I forgetting?"

"I don't know, Rabbit," answered Pooh. "Let's ask Piglet."

While Rabbit was checking on everyone, Tigger discovered Piglet's scrapbook, and showed the pictures to his friends.

"What's that tiny pink dot?" asked Tigger.

"I believe it's Piglet," answered Rabbit. He suddenly realized that Piglet wasn't there. "Where is Piglet?"

"We have to find him and make sure he's all right," said Pooh anxiously.

"But how will we find him?" asked Rabbit.

"Think, think, think," said Pooh. After he thought, he had an idea. "Since this is a book of Piglet's memories, maybe it remembers where Piglet is."

"Let's start with page one," decided Eeyore.

Page one was a picture of Owl and his house.

"Then we go to Owl's house!" said Pooh. "He has an answer for everything."

"Have you seen Piglet?" Pooh asked Owl, who was sitting on his front porch.

"Of course. In fact, I just saw him go by," Owl replied.

The others left quietly, because they knew that once Owl started talking, he could talk all day!

On page two, the scrapbook showed a picture of Kanga's house.

"Then Kanga's house is where we'll look for Piglet!" decided Rabbit.

The picture of Kanga's house reminded the friends about the time when Kanga and Roo moved into the Hundred-Acre Wood.

"You know, if I remember correctly," mused Pooh, "this story is really about Piglet."

Piglet and his friends had never seen anyone like Kanga and Roo before, and, at first, they thought the newcomers might be quite fierce.

"I tell you, we won't be safe until they're out—out of the Hundred-Acre Wood," said Rabbit.

So Rabbit devised a plan. "Pooh will distract Kanga long enough for Tigger and I to take Roo from her pouch and replace him with Piglet. Then Kanga will know that we know where Roo is, and we'll only give him back if she promises to leave the Hundred-Acre Wood!"

Their plan seemed to work. When Kanga and Roo met the friends, Pooh talked to Kanga, and Rabbit took Roo away while Tigger dropped Piglet into Kanga's pouch. Kanga bounced back home, unaware that she carried Piglet, not Roo!

While Kanga was most surprised to see Piglet at home instead of Roo, she pretended not to notice. She saw Roo playing leap-frog with Rabbit outside.

"Oh my, Roo dear, you've lost your bounce. I think it's time for your fishy oil!" Kanga said, with a big motherly smile.

"What fishy oil?" asked Piglet in dismay.

"It'll help you bounce nice and high! You don't want to grow up small and weak, like Piglet!" Kanga said.

Piglet was forced to swallow the horrible tasting fishy oil. But it made him bounce around the room, rebounding off the walls, the ceiling, the floor and the furniture. Then it was time for his bath. By the time Kanga had finished, he was so clean and fluffy he barely looked like himself.

"There's always two things you get after your bath; a cookie, and a kiss, Piglet," said Kanga with a wink. And Piglet liked both of them, and decided that Kanga was not really so fierce after all.

Piglet went skipping outside to meet Pooh and Tigger.

"Was she awfully fierce and fiercely awful?" asked Tigger.

"At first, I thought so," admitted Piglet. "But then I found out, she's very nice."

Kanga called out to them. "Hello, dears. Would you like to come in now for a little something?"

"I'd love to. I love little somethings," said Pooh.

"But what do we tell Rabbit?" wondered Tigger, as he saw Rabbit return with Roo.

"Mama! You have to see Mr. Rabbit's garden!" shouted Roo. "Thank you, Mr. Rabbit! I had fun."

"Well, I certainly enjoyed myself too, and you can call me Rabbit," said Rabbit, who had forgotten all about the plan for Kanga and Roo to leave the forest.

The friends smiled, as they remembered the happy ending to this story.

"You see, if it weren't for Piglet, we'd never have found out how nice Kanga was," Pooh said.

They continued on their way to Kanga's house.

"We're ever so worried about Piglet," Pooh told Kanga. "We lost him at the honey harvest, so we're using his book of memories to find him . . . we hope."

"Dear little Piglet," said Kanga in concern.

Roo asked if he could join in the search for Piglet. "Of course, dear," said Kanga. And so, Roo joined the others as they headed out to look for Piglet again. Pooh opened the scrapbook to page three—a picture of all of the friends at the North Pole.

"Perhaps if we told the story, the story would tell us how to get there," said Pooh.

"Don't forget the part about Piglet!" Roo reminded them.

"Roo's right," said Tigger. "It really is a story about Piglet, isn't it?"

This story started when Christopher Robin told his friends they were going on an expedition.

"It's when you go off to find a thing," Christopher Robin explained to Pooh, Piglet and Tigger.

"What are we going to find, Christopher Robin?" asked Pooh.

"The North Pole," he answered. "And if you see the North Pole, shout 'Eureka!'"

They marched off through the Hundred-Acre Wood, and Eeyore, Rabbit, Kanga, Roo and Owl joined them.

Along the way, Roo fell into the stream. "Pooh! I'm swimming!" he called excitedly.

Everyone panicked, trying to think of a way to rescue Roo. But Roo was happily swimming in the stream, floating with the current.

Tigger fell in, but couldn't reach Roo. "Piglet!" he called. "Stay here out of the way while we save Roo. We don't want to have to rescue two little guys."

Eeyore, Pooh, Rabbit and Tigger all tried to save Roo without any success. "You can rescue me now," called Roo. "I'm getting kind of tired."

It was Piglet who found a long stick in the grass, and with a great effort, managed to lower it over a rock, into the water in front of Roo. Just as Roo grabbed the stick, Piglet jumped on the other end, and Roo and the stick flew into the air.

Piglet caught the stick, gave it to Pooh, and rushed off to catch Roo. Roo landed safely in Kanga's arms.

"Pooh Bear, where did you find that stick?" asked Christopher Robin, as he joined everyone.

"Well, I was standing here without a stick . . . and then I had a stick, so maybe the stick found me," Pooh replied.

Christopher Robin addressed his friends. "Assembled Adventurers, the expedition is over! Pooh has discovered the North Pole!"

"This?" said Pooh, looking in amazement at the stick in his hands.

"That!" said Christopher Robin.

"Eureka!" shouted Pooh.

"I always like that story. It has such a lovely end," said Pooh as he remembered the North Pole expedition.

"Piglet was so brave, for someone so small," said Roo.

Just then, Roo noticed Piglet's scarf, caught on a fence post.

"Oh my, you know, Piglet's scarf never goes anywhere without Piglet," Pooh said.

"This is more serious than I thought," said Rabbit, worriedly. "Maybe he's in grave danger. And now he's out there somewhere . . . with this storm blowing in . . ."

Rabbit looked at Piglet's scrapbook on page four. "Pooh Corner, remember?" he asked the others.

"Is this a story about Piglet, too?" asked Roo.

"Why, yes, Roo, it is," replied Pooh, "He just seems to be the hero of every story."

This story begins when Piglet and Pooh were walking in the snow.

"I was just thinking," Piglet began, "about how you have a house, and I have a house, and Rabbit and Owl and Christopher Robin all have houses, but poor Eeyore has nothing."

"Well," said Pooh, "that's certainly something we can think about." He thought for a bit. "I've got it! We'll build Eeyore a house of his own," Pooh decided.

"That's a wonderful idea, Pooh! But where shall we build it?" asked Piglet.

"Right here!" said Pooh. "Because this is where I thought of it! And since this is where I thought of it, we shall call this place . . . 'Pooh Corner!'"

"'Pooh Corner?'" said Piglet disappointedly. "But . . . Pooh, I was thinking along with you."

"Yes, that's true, Piglet. We could call this place 'Pooh-and-Piglet Corner' . . ." reflected Pooh.

Piglet smiled.

"If 'Pooh Corner' didn't sound better," Pooh continued, "which it does, being smaller and more like a corner; so 'Pooh Corner' it is."

Before Piglet had time to protest, Tigger came bouncing up to them. He and Pooh and Piglet began to build Eeyore a house of sticks.

But the house kept falling down.

"I suspect something's wrong with these sticks," said Tigger. "All we wanted was for Eeyore to have his own house."

"You know," thought Pooh, "Eeyore could come live with me."

So Tigger and Pooh deserted the pile of sticks, leaving Piglet behind, and went to tell Eeyore and Christopher Robin the news.

But before Pooh and Tigger could explain their offer to Eeyore, Piglet rushed up, using a pair of sticks as stilts to move through the snow.

"Eeyore's house is over there," Piglet said. "Come on, I'll show you."

So Piglet led Pooh, Christopher Robin, Tigger and Eeyore to a hill. Everyone stopped in surprise. There was a house of sticks, beautifully built with a little snowman in front.

"Welcome home, Eeyore," said Piglet proudly. "I put up a sign so you'll always know where it is."

The sign said "Pooh Corner" and had a little drawing of Pooh's face on it.

Eeyore was very happy.

"And that is how Piglet got the idea that Eeyore should have his own house," explained Pooh, as they looked at Piglet's scrapbook.

The friends called out to Piglet as they crossed a bridge. There was no answer.

"Hey! I've just got a tiggeriffic idea. Let's see where the book ends and go there!" Tigger said to his friends.

"No, no," said Rabbit. "If we do this in an orderly manner, we'll find him much quicker."

But as Rabbit and Tigger began fighting over the scrapbook and the best way to find Piglet, the book ripped apart in their hands and fell over the bridge into the water below.

"There goes our map," said Rabbit sadly.

"And Piglet's memories," said Pooh.

The friends made their way back to Piglet's house to keep themselves warm. Roo and Pooh began to draw a face of Piglet on the window. Then the others joined in, and started drawing with paper and crayons. They drew pictures of Piglet and his many adventures.

"We've got to go get Piglet!" Roo insisted. And so they went out into the dark and stormy night.

They found pictures from Piglet's scrapbook, scattered along the riverbank.

"Maybe we can put Piglet's scrapbook back together," suggested Tigger.

"Then we can find him in no time!" said Pooh.

They hurried about, collecting all the pictures. And then they saw the cover, caught on the end of a log jutting out over the cliff, with a raging waterfall underneath it.

Rabbit began to think of a plan to rescue the scrapbook cover, but Pooh had already begun to climb the tree.

"I'm just getting Piglet's memories," Pooh called, as he carefully moved along the fallen log.

But he slipped through a hole in the log and was caught on a branch below.

"Oh, bother," said Pooh, as he dangled over the waterfall.

The friends joined together to form a rescue rope, stretching out over the log to reach out to Pooh. But they were too short.

"The rescue rope isn't rescuing," Pooh called.

"We need a little bit more!" said Tigger.

"We just need a little help," Roo said.

"Who's small enough?" wondered Eeyore.

"Oh dear! Who can help?" Rabbit asked.

Suddenly, Piglet was there, stepping over each person until he reached Pooh.

"Piglet!" cried the others in relief.

"My friends need me!" said Piglet determinedly, and he reached out into the hole and took hold of Pooh's hand, pulling him onto the log.

But the log split in two and half of the log plummeted into the waterfall below, along with Piglet's scrapbook cover. Rabbit, Eeyore, Tigger and Roo landed back on the river bank safely. But there was no sign of Pooh or Piglet.

"We never got to tell Piglet how we feel about him," said Rabbit sadly.

"Or Pooh," added Roo.

"Should have told them when we had the chance," realized Eeyore.

But Pooh and Piglet reached the riverbank safely.

"Pooh! Piglet!" the others called.

"We're so glad to see you," Tigger shouted.

"Glad to see me?" asked Piglet.

"Yeah, we've been following your memories all over the Hundred-Acre Wood, and they led us right to you," Roo explained.

"Too bad they're all floating down the river," Eeyore said, as he watched Piglet's pictures beneath them.

"The scrapbook's not that important," said Piglet.

"But it showed us the great things you've done," said Pooh. And the others decided to take Piglet back to his house to show him.

Piglet stood at his front door and gasped. There before him were many drawings by his friends, showing the grand things Piglet had done.

"Oh my!" Piglet said in amazement.

He looked at a picture of himself in armor. "Is that me?" he asked in astonishment.

"That's you," replied Pooh.

"I'm so big!" said Piglet.

"I'd say this calls for a celebration," called Pooh. So the friends organized a party for Piglet.

But Pooh had one more surprise. He led Piglet out the door and took him to Eeyore's house. The sign now said "Pooh and Piglet Corner" and had a drawing of Piglet as well as Pooh.

"It's the least we could do for a very small Piglet who's done such very big things," said Pooh. Piglet smiled.

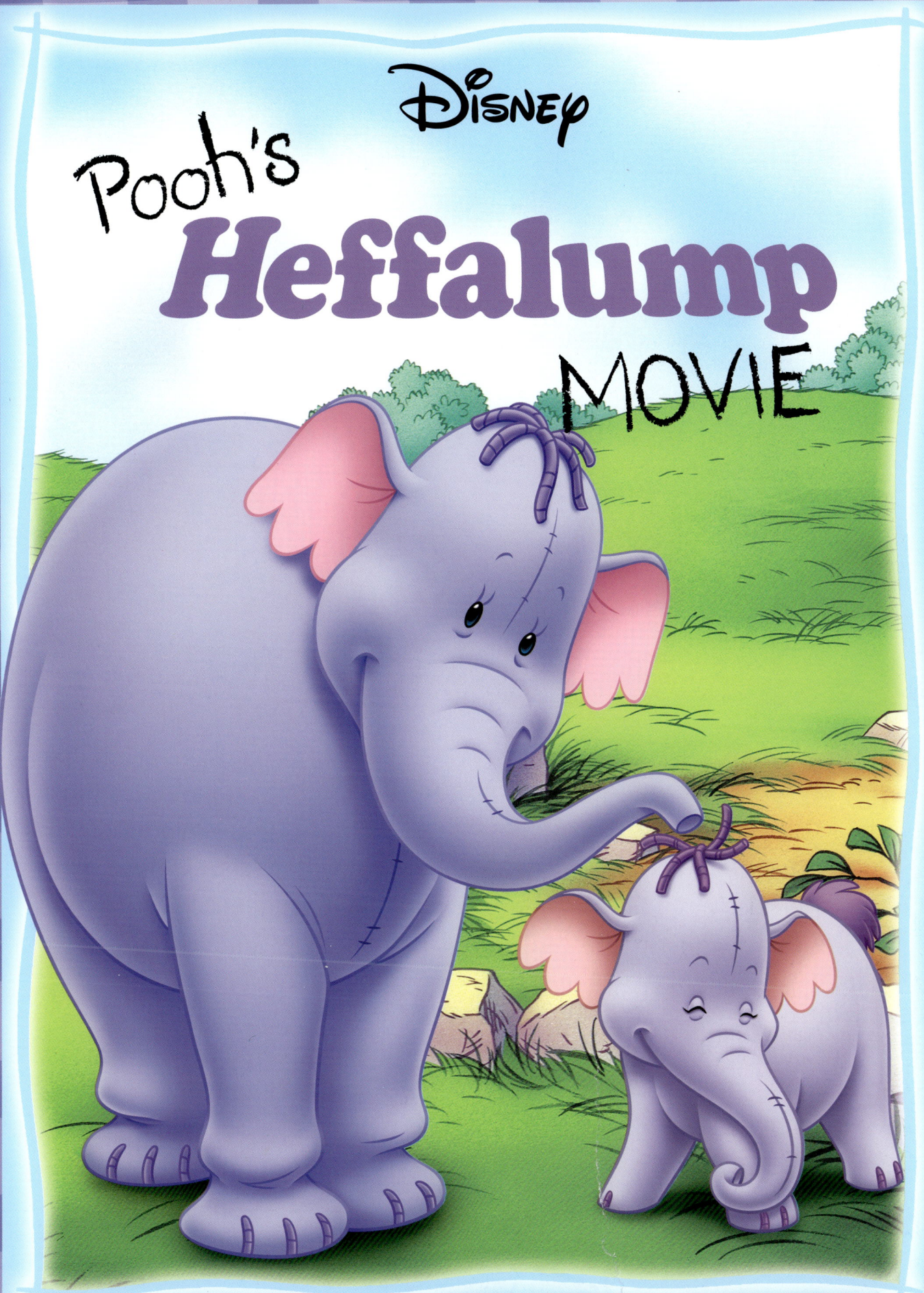

Early one morning, an alarmingly loud and frightening trumpeting noise was heard throughout the usually tranquil Hundred-Acre Wood.

Pooh was dreaming of honey when he heard this strange sound. He woke up with a fright, and fell head first into the jar of honey next to his bed.

"Oh bother!" he said, from inside the honeypot.

Piglet was sleeping peacefully when he too, was woken by the unfamiliar noise.

"Oh, d-d-dear!" he stammered, and ran out of his house in a panic, straight into a sheet hanging on his laundry line. "It's got me!" he shouted.

Asleep in his hammock, Tigger woke up when he heard the terrible noise. He jumped up and crashed into a picture hanging on the wall.

Only Roo was excited when he heard the strange trumpeting noise. "Mama!" he called to Kanga. "Did you hear that sound?"

Pooh, Piglet, Tigger and Roo ran to Rabbit's house.

"He'll know what to do!" said Piglet.

They pounded on Rabbit's door. Rabbit opened the door, still half asleep, wearing a pink bathrobe with curlers in his ears.

"It came at me in the dark," moaned Piglet.

"I heard this really neat sound," cried Roo.

"It was terrible," said Pooh.

"There was a zillion of them," insisted Tigger.

"Well! What we have here is a mystery—of the most mysterious kind!" Rabbit declared.

The mystery became even more mysterious, as just then, Roo discovered a huge footprint. The friends were horrified.

"Rabbit," asked Pooh in a puzzled kind of way, "what sort of creature do you suppose would be attached to a foot that big?"

"There's only one thing it could be . . ." answered Rabbit, ". . . a heffalump!" His friends gasped in shock.

"What's a heffalump?" asked Roo curiously.

The others did their best to describe this frightful creature.

"It's got a spiky tail!" said Tigger.

"And sharp claws," added Rabbit.

Everyone agreed heffalumps were big and wide and very, very mean.

"And they live right over there! Heffalump Hollow!" said Rabbit nervously, pointing out to the other side of the Hundred-Acre Wood.

"Let's go get them!" shouted Roo, very excited at the thought of these strange and fearsome creatures.

"Capture a heffalump?" asked Rabbit scornfully. "Impossible!"

"It'd be an adventure!" said Roo persuasively.

"Hmm," thought Rabbit. "The first heffalump expedition in history. Oh, splendid idea!"

"But how does one capture a heffalump?" Pooh inquired.

"Come back with your equipment and I'll show you how it's done," said Rabbit with authority.

The others went away, and then came back with all sorts of interesting, although not necessarily useful, equipment.

Rabbit ignored everything Pooh, Tigger and Piglet brought, but was impressed with Roo's rope.

Rabbit instructed his friends how to throw a rope to catch a heffalump. "Say in a firm voice," he told them, "'In the name of Hundred-Acre Wood, I capture you.'"

"I did it!" shouted Roo, as he expertly threw his rope around the practice barrel. "Let's go get them!"

"Ah, just a moment, Roo. A heffalump expedition is fraught with danger. You're simply too young. You could get hurt," Rabbit said.

"But I . . ." Roo began.

"Rooooo! Time to come home!" called Kanga, from a distance.

Roo reluctantly went home to Kanga.

Before he went to bed, Roo told Kanga about the horrible heffalumps.

"I'm grown up enough to catch a heffalump, aren't I, Mama?" Roo asked Kanga.

"You're growing up very fast, indeed, dear," Kanga said.

"Do you think I could grow up by tomorrow morning?" asked Roo hopefully.

"You know, dear, growing up doesn't happen all at once. It takes its own time," Kanga said wisely as she kissed Roo good night.

In the morning, before anyone else was awake, Roo had already left for his own heffalump expedition, armed with his rope.

"I just know I could catch one . . ." he said to himself.

"Ah, yes, a perfect morning for catching heffalumps!" said Rabbit, as the group set off. "With courage, cunning and superior tactics, we'll be home by tea time."

But as they approached the fence dividing Heffalump Hollow from the rest of the Hundred-Acre Wood, it seemed to the friends that the birds had stopped singing and everything appeared a little darker, with strange shadows.

"Oh my," muttered Piglet. "I believe that what's over there doesn't look quite as friendly as what's over here."

But they climbed over the fence to Heffalump Hollow, and continued their heffalump hunt.

Roo also noticed that the Wood seemed a little scarier with darker shadows and strange noises. He saw an old mill with a large wooden door, and nervously moved in, holding his rope tightly.

"Hello? Is anyone there?" he called out bravely through the dim, dusty darkness.

A dark shape brushed past Roo. "You're it!" said a voice, laughing in the shadows. Roo screamed.

Something tapped him again. "Now you got to catch me!" the voice said.

Roo leapt up in fright. "I tagged you, so you're 'it,'" explained the dark shape very patiently. "Don't you want to play?"

Roo stuttered as he tried to think of an excuse. "I've got to catch a heffalump!" he said. The dark shape giggled, and tumbled out of the mill, pushing Roo along with him. "You can catch me. I'm a heffalump!"

Out in the bright sunlight, Roo could see that the dark shape was certainly something he'd never seen before!

"But . . . you can't be . . ." Roo said in astonishment, looking at this strange creature. "If you're a heffalump, then where are your horns and spiky tail? Are you sure you're a heffalump?"

"My Mummy says I am," giggled the heffalump.

"Well, if you're a heffalump, then, in the name of the Hundred-Acre Wood—I capture you!" said Roo, as he twirled his rope and flung it over the heffalump's neck.

The heffalump thought this was a wonderful game and scampered off, pulling Roo, who was holding onto the other end of the rope, behind him.

"Stop!" cried Roo desperately, as the heffalump dragged him through some bushes. "You've got to come with me," he insisted.

"Why?" asked the heffalump.

"Because I'm a grown-up," Roo said proudly.

"Wow! You're a grown-up?" asked the heffalump, impressed. "You must have your own call then. I haven't found mine yet. My Mum said I'll find it when I grow up," the heffalump explained, as he lifted his trunk and tried to blow a loud trumpet. It didn't sound very loud or strong.

"Well, growing up takes a long time," said Roo knowingly. "It took me just about forever."

Just then, they heard a loud trumpeting sound, much stronger than the heffalump's attempt.

"Got to go now!" said the heffalump cheerfully. "My Mummy's calling."

"Don't go yet. Let's go see my friends first, then you can go," begged Roo.

"Ok. But as soon as we're done, I've got to go," said the heffalump.

As they hopped and bounced through the forest, the heffalump introduced himself. "My name is Heffridge Trumpler Brompet Heffalump the Fourth."

"Whoa . . . how do you remember all of that?" asked Roo.

"I can't . . . so everybody calls me Lumpy," replied the heffalump with a giggle.

Meanwhile, Pooh, Piglet, Tigger and Rabbit heard the same loud frightening trumpeting noise they had heard before.

They shrieked, and dived into a hollow log.

"I suggest a retreat to another part of the Wood!" said Rabbit.

Roo hopped through the fence leading to his side of the Hundred Acre Wood. But Lumpy stopped. He looked terrified.

"I'm not supposed to go in that part of the woods," Lumpy dropped his voice to a frightened whisper. "Scary things live there."

"Huh?" said Roo in surprise. "That's where I live. There aren't any scary things there."

"There's a stripey thing that bounces. Then it pounces!" Lumpy insisted.

"No, that's Tigger. He's great," laughed Roo.

"There's this little pink monster that squeals and shakes all the time," Lumpy continued.

"Oh, you're wrong about Piglet, too. He wouldn't hurt a fly," Roo explained.

"And then there's the loud thing!" said Lumpy. "And it's got long ears and it yells at everybody."

"Yeah . . . you're kind of right about Rabbit. But he's ok . . . once you get to know him," Roo admitted. "But my friends aren't scary."

"Promise?" asked Lumpy.

"Promise," said Roo.

So Lumpy wriggled his way through the fence.

They made their way to Pooh's house, but there was nobody there. Lumpy sniffed curiously at all the honeypots. Then his long trunk plopped the honey out and right into his mouth.

"My Mum usually makes me a snack about now," he explained as he ate all the honey.

"Oh well, I guess Pooh won't mind," said Roo. "But we better leave before we break something."

They tried to tiptoe out carefully, but when they closed the door several honeypots crashed to the floor.

There was no one at Rabbit's house either. But Lumpy found Rabbit's garden, and happily munched his way through Rabbit's watermelon.

Roo had a mischievous idea. He started spitting watermelon seeds at Lumpy. But Lumpy loaded his trunk with seeds and fired them back at Roo. Roo soon realized that Lumpy was very good at firing with his trunk!

Roo and Lumpy had a wonderful time playing games in Rabbit's garden. After a little while, the friends surveyed the damage to Rabbit's garden, and each other.

"My Mum's not going to like this, Rooty-toot," said Lumpy ruefully.

"Yeah. My Mom neither, Lumpster," agreed Roo.

"Lumpster . . ." said Roo. "You're not captured any more." And Roo removed the rope around Lumpy's neck.

The fearless heffalump hunters—Tigger, Rabbit, Pooh and Piglet—ran from Heffalump Hollow, and found themselves back in the familiar part of the Hundred-Acre Wood.

"Well, well . . . all in all, a successful heffalump expedition," noted Rabbit.

"Are you sure, Rabbit?" asked Pooh.

"Well, certainly!" he replied with conviction. "Just look around, you don't see any heffalumps, do you?"

But just as Rabbit looked around, he saw giant heffalump footprints leading to Pooh's house!

The friends stood in Pooh's doorway and looked at the broken honeypots.

"Oh bother," said Pooh in a resigned sort of way. "I don't think it's successful any more."

Rabbit was not so calm when he saw the heffalump had been in his garden.

"The heffalumps are amongst us!" he cried, frightened.

"It's an invasion!" cried Tigger.

"Run for your lives!" squealed Piglet.

"Hide your honey!" called Pooh.

"Trapped! We're trapped!" shouted Piglet.

Rabbit stopped. "That's it! We need traps! Everywhere!"

So they built a number of unusual traps.

"I'd like to see a heffalump breach these defenses!" said Rabbit proudly, as the friends stood back to survey the results of their hard work.

Roo and Lumpy were still playing in the forest when they heard Mama Heffalump calling to Lumpy from a great distance.

"Oh, no! We forgot your Mom!" said Roo anxiously. "I'll help you find her."

But Lumpy and Roo couldn't find Lumpy's mom.

Lumpy tried his call but it was no use. It wasn't loud enough. "I want my Mum," he said, sniffing.

"Me too," said Roo. "Wait . . . my Mama. She'll know what to do!"

So Roo and Lumpy went back to find Kanga.

Kanga was also looking for Roo. She hopped through the Hundred-Acre Wood, calling out to him. But she tripped over a rope, and Tigger's net trap fell over her.

"Oh my goodness!" cried Kanga. "What's all this for?" she asked, as the friends helped her out of the trap.

"We've built traps to catch the heffalump," explained Piglet.

Finally, Roo saw Kanga and his friends in the distance. Everything was going to be fine now. He and Lumpy moved forward, both of them holding onto one end of the rope.

"Roo!" cried Kanga, very relieved to see him.

"This is Lumpy! He's a heffalump!" introduced Roo.

The friends, except for Kanga, were shocked, then frightened.

"Stop him!" called Tigger.

Roo was surprised, and Lumpy was terrified. The others charged towards him.

Lumpy ran away into the trees and disappeared.

Roo raced after his friend, following his footprints, until he found Lumpy, caught in Pooh's bamboo cage.

Lumpy was crying. "You said they wouldn't be scary," he sniffed.

"Oh, Lumpy, I am so sorry," Roo said sadly.

He heard his friends calling out to him, and knew he had to get Lumpy out of there quickly. Roo climbed up to the top of the cage, and with a big effort, managed to undo the knot that held the bamboo stalks together. They fell away instantly.

Lumpy reached up with his trunk, and gently hugged Roo.

But the others found them, and saw Lumpy with his trunk coiled around Roo.

"The heffalump's got him!" said Pooh.

And the heffalump hunters charged forward, brandishing lassoes.

"Wait!" shouted Kanga.

But it was too late.

"In the name of the Hundred-Acre Wood . . . I capture you!" they shouted, and the lassoes landed around Lumpy's neck.

"No!" shouted Roo. "Let him go! You're scaring him!"

"We were wrong about heffalumps!" insisted Roo. "They're not big and scary. Lumpy's my friend. So you've got to uncapture him."

"He gets afraid," Roo explained.

"Oh," said Piglet—he understood what it was like to be afraid. He released his rope from around Lumpy's neck.

"And he likes honey," Roo said.

"Oh," said Pooh. Honey was something he understood. He took his rope off Lumpy.

"He's even learning how to bounce!" Roo continued.

"Oh," said Tigger, who knew that bouncing was what Tiggers did best. He undid his rope around Lumpy.

Only Rabbit held on to his rope. He looked around at the others, and finally gave in, releasing his rope around Lumpy.

But Lumpy was still scared, and he slowly backed away. He didn't realize that there was a steep slope behind him. He lost his footing and fell backwards into a huge pile of fallen logs, with twisted branches and roots.

"Lumpy!" cried Roo, as he grabbed one of the ropes and went after Lumpy.

Lumpy managed to grab onto a tree root as Roo was flung off the end of the rope.

The friends panicked. Roo had been tossed into the heap of fallen logs, where he slipped beneath the twisted branches.

Kanga and Tigger tried to pull some of the logs off Roo but it was no use, the logs were too heavy and the branches and roots were entwined so tightly that it was impossible to separate them.

"Roo, I've got an idea!" shouted Lumpy. He ran to the edge of the fallen logs, and started to call. His trumpeting was very weak. But he kept trying.

Finally, there was a loud and triumphant "Taroot, taroot!"

Lumpy had found his call!

He held up his ears listening intently, and then he heard an answer. It was his mother, returning his call.

"Mummy!" Lumpy cried in excitement.

"Mummy?" The friends weren't too sure they wanted to see another heffalump.

Mama Heffalump came crashing through the forest, trumpeting. The friends cowered in terror, all except Kanga.

"Heffridge Trumpler Brompet Heffalump the Fourth! Where have you been?" she spoke crossly to Lumpy.

Then she relented. "Oh, my little darling, I've been worried sick." She wound her trunk around Lumpy and gave him a tight hug.

"I'm ok, Mummy, but my friend Roo's in trouble. Can't you save him?" Lumpy begged.

Lumpy led his mother to the hole with the fallen logs. Then she took control.

"Roo, can you hear me, love? Now don't be frightened. I'm Lumpy's Mummy."

The fallen logs creaked alarmingly as Mama Heffalump used her great strength to throw the logs away, one after the other. She worked tirelessly, moving closer and closer to Roo.

She slunk her long trunk through an opening in the logs, and reached out to Roo. The others watched anxiously.

And then Mama Heffalump emerged from the logs with Roo wrapped around her trunk. She passed Roo back to Kanga.

"Mama!" shouted Roo, as he clung to Kanga.

"Roo! I was so worried," cried Kanga.

"Thanks, Mrs. Heffalump," said Roo.

She winked at him and turned towards Lumpy, who trumpeted joyfully.

"Oh, Lumpy, you found your call," Mama Heffalump said proudly.

The others watched in amazement.

"Well, would you look at that. Heffalumps don't have spiky tails after all," said Tigger in wonder.

Rabbit approached Lumpy cautiously. "Can you ever forgive us? We've acted very badly," he apologized.

"That's ok, Long Ears," laughed Lumpy.

"I have to go home now," Lumpy said to Roo, at his mother's nudging.

"Goodbye, Lumpster," said Roo, as he hugged his new friend goodbye.

"Goodbye, Rooty-toot," said Lumpy.

Then both Roo and Lumpy turned to their mothers and said at the same time, "Could we please stay up just a bit longer?"

Their mothers smiled, winked at each other, and agreed. Roo and Lumpy laughed, and dashed through the Wood, chasing each other.

Pooh looked thoughtful. "You know we never really did capture a heffalump that day. It was more like Lumpy captured all of us."

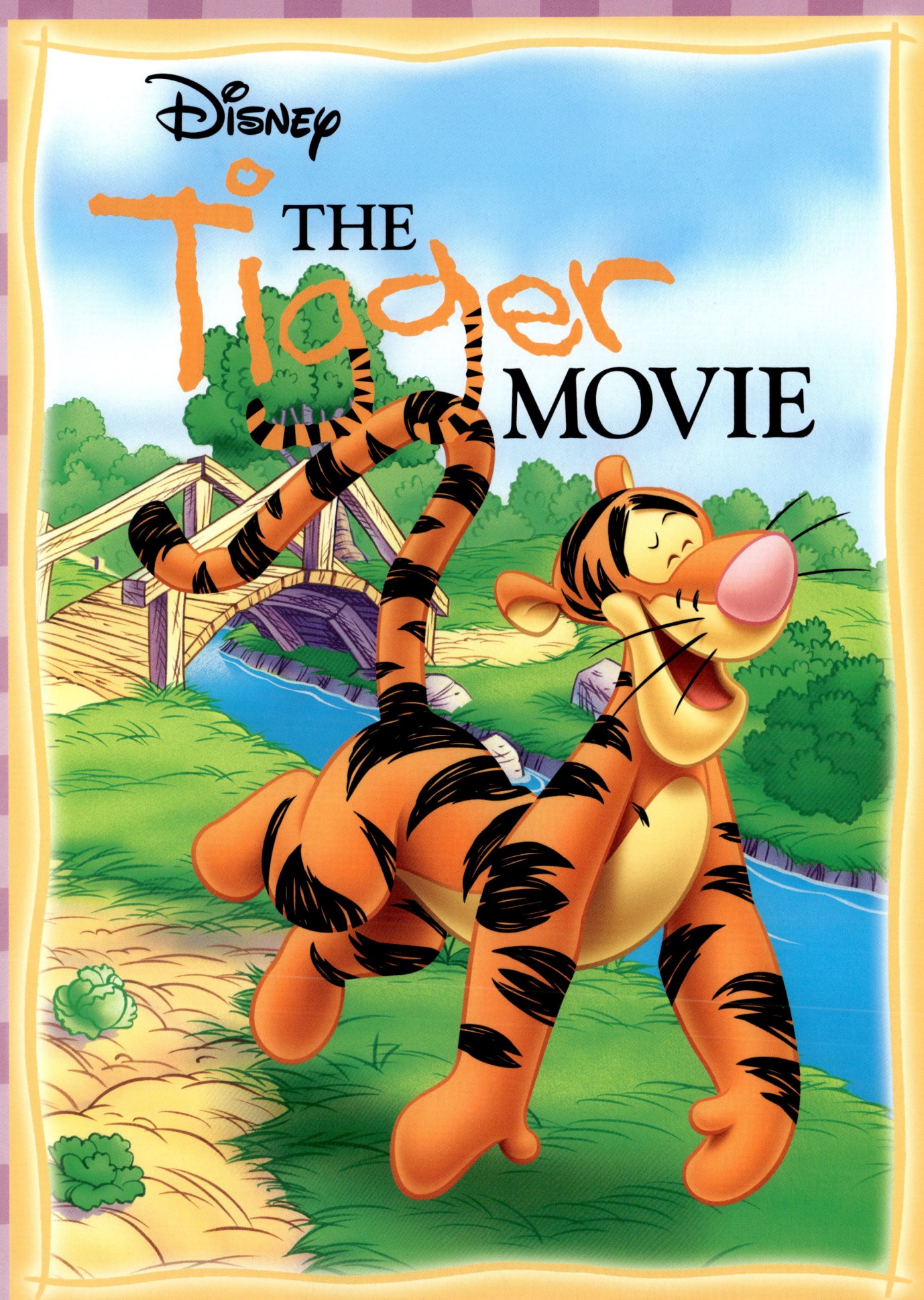

Like most small boys, Christopher Robin had toy animals to play with; and together, they had many remarkable adventures in an enchanted place called the Hundred-Acre Wood. But of all his animal friends, Christopher Robin's very best friend was a bear named Winnie-the-Pooh or Pooh for short.

This bothered Tigger a bit. "Seems to me that most of these stories are about that silly old bear," he said.

He wanted a story about himself— "someone who's extremely fascinating!"

Now, there are many wonderful things about tiggers. They're bouncy and jumpy, but the best thing of all—there's no one else quite like them!

One day, Pooh was at home counting his honeypots. Suddenly, Tigger bounced through the door and right into him, sending the honeypots tumbling everywhere.

"Say, you want to go bouncing with me?" Tigger asked enthusiastically, as he tried to remove a sticky honeypot from his foot.

"Well, I would go bouncing with you, Tigger, except that I must count all these honeypots to be sure that I have enough for winter," Pooh replied.

"What do these Pooh Bears like about this icky sticky stuff anyway?" Tigger asked, and he bounced out the door.

Next, Tigger bounced into Piglet's house. "Hi Piglet, old pal! What say you and I do a little bouncing together?"

Piglet was flustered. "Bouncing? Oh, my, I haven't enough firewood to last the winter, and . . ."

"Oh well, then. Got to be bouncing along!" replied Tigger, and he left.

Kanga was sweeping the leaves in front of her door when Tigger arrived at her house.

"Why, hello there, and good morning, Mrs. Kanga, ma'am," Tigger greeted her. "You wouldn't happen to be interested in doing a bit of bouncing with me, would you?"

"Well, I'm afraid I have just too much to do this morning, dear," Kanga replied.

A hopeful little face appeared at the window behind Kanga and Tigger. It was Roo.

Roo came running down the stairs. "Tigger!" he shouted, but Tigger bounced away without seeing him. Roo sighed.

Tigger sat forlornly on a large boulder on top of a cliff. He asked himself sadly, "I wonder why nobody wants to bounce with me?"

"Oh well. What am I talking about? There's plenty of others that I haven't even asked yet!" In an instant, he was back to his usual tiggerish self.

He leapt off the boulder, landed on a small tree, and headed into the woods. But the tree sprang back when Tigger's weight was released and pushed the boulder over the cliff.

Eeyore had just walked outside when, a second later, a large boulder fell on his house, crushing it completely.

Pooh, Piglet, Rabbit, Kanga, and Roo gathered around poor Eeyore.

"Ahem! Your attention, please!" said Rabbit importantly. "I have officially completed the plans for removing this boulder and restoring to Eeyore his happy home."

"No need to bother on my account," said Eeyore gloomily.

Under Rabbit's directions, the friends put Rabbit's Rock Remover together. Rabbit organized them into position.

But the stitches on Pooh's back began to pop, as he strained to pull down on a lever. He released it, sending Piglet flying. Roo was thrown up into the air, and Eeyore was slammed into the top of the pulley.

As the friends tried to figure out what went wrong, Tigger jumped in, sending Rabbit and his plans flying. "Anyone up for a little bouncing?" Tigger asked.

Rabbit said, from underneath Tigger, "No bouncing! Just look at all this work we have to do!"

"What? Moving that old thing? Not a problem. All you need is a little bouncing!" Tigger said confidently.

Tigger studied the boulder very carefully, noting one small spot on it. Then he twisted his whole body, including his tail and released himself into the air. He spun into a very powerful bounce, propelling himself from tree to tree and then headed for the very spot he had found. This launched Rabbit's Rock Remover and the boulder with it. But everyone else was caught up too.

The boulder rolled along the ground with considerable speed, dragging the Remover and everyone behind it until they all landed in a stream.

"Now that's out of the way, who's up for a little bouncing?" Tigger asked cheerfully.

Rabbit was furious. "Everything's ruined, and all you can think about is bouncing?"

"But that's what tiggers do best," Tigger said, looking around at the others for support. His friends were too busy wiping the mud from themselves.

Tigger was confused.

Piglet tried to explain. "We really can't bounce like tiggers, anyway, because, uh . . ."

"We're not tiggers," said Pooh, sadly.

Tigger was disheartened at his friends' words. He turned and walked away, hanging his head.

Tigger drifted off slowly through the Wood without a single bounce.

"Who needs those other fellows anyhow? Usually, I'm happy because I'm the only tigger, but now I'm kinda lonely for somebody like me."

Roo finally caught up to him. "Don't be sad, Tigger," he said. "Why don't you go bouncing? That will cheer you up!"

"No one to bounce with, Roo boy," Tigger replied sadly.

"Well, what about another tigger?" Roo suggested.

"Another . . . tigger? No, it's impossible. I'm the only one."

"But aren't there other tiggers? Don't you have a family somewhere?"

"A family full of tiggers? Can you imagine such a thing? We'd be bouncing morning, noon, and night!" Tigger said in amazement.

It was a windy, blustery day when Tigger and Roo went to visit Owl.
"You wish to find your family? A most noble quest, indeed!" said Owl, nodding wisely as he poured tea for Tigger and Roo.

Owl droned on and on ". . . one must first look up one's family tree."

Tigger gasped. "My family tree! Why didn't I think of thinking that?"

And so began Tigger's grand search for his family tree. He searched high and low. He searched near and far.

"Tigger," panted Roo, trying to keep up with him. "Tigger, how are you going to know which tree is your family tree?"

"Why, that's obvious, Roo boy!" Tigger replied. "My Tigger family tree has got to be the biggest, hugest, and most gigantical tree in the entire Hundred-Acre Wood! And besides, it'll be all stripey, just like yours truly!"

Tigger was discouraged. He couldn't find a single stripey tigger tree anywhere. He and Roo went back to Tigger's house to look for clues. Tigger began pulling things out of a barrel, looking for anything that might lead him to his family.

"Just think!" Tigger pondered. "If there are other tiggers, we could all bounce the Whoop-de-Dooper Loop-de-Looper Alley-Ooper Bounce! Because it's the bounce that tiggers do best!"

Roo was very impressed by the sound of this complicated bounce. "The Whoopdie . . . what kind of bounce?"

"The hardest bounce of them all, that only the very best bouncers can bounce," Tigger boasted.

"I could bounce it," said Roo shyly. "If you could teach me . . ."

"That's ridickerous!" Tigger said in shock. "It's a very powerful bounce and it's only for professional bouncers," he insisted.

"But I'm a really good bouncer," protested Roo. "I could do the whooper-dooper . . . um . . . the looper-duper . . ."

Tigger cut in. "You can't bounce the bounce if you can't even pronounce the bounce. Repeat after Tigger—the Whoop-de-Dooper Loop-de-Looper Alley-Ooper Bounce!"

Tigger showed Roo the Bounce—he wound himself up, spun himself around, whizzed through the air, propelled himself across the room, bounced off the walls, flew out the window, and then back in again, and landed before Roo with a flourish. Roo was in awe of his friend.

Roo immediately began to wind himself up like Tigger, preparing for the Bounce. He flipped around a hammock, spun around on a record player, but then smashed into an open closet, and tottered out, feeling a little stunned.

"Think you let it a little loose," Tigger advised kindly. But then he noticed that Roo was twisted up with a heart-shaped, gold locket.

"This is the exact thingamabob I was looking for!" Tigger cried in excitement. "And it must have a picture of my tigger family inside it!"

With great apprehension, Tigger and Roo looked inside the locket.
"Empty," said Tigger sadly. "Completely tiggerless."
"Maybe there's another way to reach them?" Roo had an idea. "A letter! Why don't you write them a letter?"
So Tigger wrote:

Dear tiggers,
Greetings and salutations. Please drop by any old time, on account of my house is your house, and vicey-versey.
Love, Tigger

Tigger and Roo sat forlornly by the mail box, while the snow fell down. There was no response to Tigger's letter.

Tigger sniffled and said, "I might as well face it. There aren't any other tiggers."

"But isn't that the wonderful thing about tiggers, being the only one?" Roo reminded him.

Tigger agreed. But then he said sadly to himself, "Yep. I'm the only one."

Roo wished he could do something to make Tigger feel better.

At Owl's house, everyone gathered around the desk—Kanga, Roo, Pooh, Piglet, and Eeyore. Roo had asked Owl to write a letter to Tigger.

"Dear Tigger," he began. "Just a note to say . . . what shall it say?" Owl asked the friends.

"Dress warmly," suggested Kanga, as she wrapped a scarf around Roo's neck.

"Eat well," thought Pooh, as he ate out of his honeypot.

"Stay safe and sound," advised Piglet timidly.

"Keep smiling," muttered Eeyore.

"We're always there for you," Roo added.

"Wishing you all the best. Signed, Your Family," Owl finished the letter.

The next morning, everyone was awakened early by Tigger.

"Look at what I got! A letter! From my very own tigger family! I knew I had one!" Tigger was so excited, he could barely keep still.

His friends smiled secretly at each other.

"A great big tigger family, full of uncles and aunties and grand-tiggers and second cousin tiggers, and they're all just like me! And they're coming to see me tomorrow!" Tigger shouted joyfully.

The others gasped. "Now where did it say that exactly?" Owl asked.

"Exactly nowhere," Tigger replied, "but us tiggers can read between the lines!"

Tigger was very busy preparing for his family. He added a family room to his house and decorated it for their reunion. There were tigger stripes everywhere—streamers, balloons, posters and a huge cake.

In turn, Pooh, Kanga, Piglet, Eeyore, and Owl tried to explain about the letter. "Uh, Tigger, there is a really important matter . . ." But Tigger was too busy organizing his family reunion to listen.

It was Roo who had the brilliant idea. All of them—Pooh, Piglet, Eeyore, Kanga, Roo, and Owl—were to dress up as tiggers, and visit Tigger, pretending to be his family.

"What we have to do is act real tiggery. We have to do a lot of bouncing and say a lot of tigger stuff," Roo told them all.

"But we don't know how to be a tigger," Pooh said sadly.

"Yes we do. Tigger will think we're his family if we just act happy," Roo explained.

The others were convinced.

Tigger paced frantically in his house. "I wonder where they could be?"

He flung open the door, ready to go searching for his family, when suddenly; there they were, standing at the door.

But of course, it was really Pooh, Piglet, Owl, Eeyore, Kanga, and Roo, dressed in their tiger costumes.

"Is it, is it, is it really you, my very own one and only family?" Tigger cried in surprise.

Roo said, "Gee, it's nice to have all us tiggers getting together like this. Huh?"

Roo and Tigger decided they needed to bounce the Whoop-de-Dooper Loop-de-Looper Alley-Ooper Bounce. Tigger gestured for Roo to go first.

Roo did a great job, remembering all of Tigger's instructions, but he did land headfirst in a closet. Tigger was confused—a tigger, crashing into the closet while bouncing? But when Roo popped out of the closet, his mask became loose.

"Roo, what are you doing, impersonating a tigger?" Tigger asked suspiciously. He turned to the others and began to pull their masks off.

"We only wanted to help, Tigger," explained Pooh.

Tigger was very upset. "Oh, now I understand. It was all a big joke. Well that's alright, because somewhere out there, there's a Tigger Family Tree, and I'm going to find them."

"Ta ta forever," he declared. Tigger slammed the door behind him, and walked out into the howling blizzard.

Rabbit, Pooh, Piglet, Roo, and Eeyore decided to go into the blizzard to find Tigger. They plunged deeper and deeper into the snow, all of them terribly cold and wet. They called and called for Tigger, but there was no answer.

Meanwhile, Tigger was out in the blizzard too, desperately searching for his tigger family. Suddenly, there in front of him was "the biggest, hugest, and most gigantical stripedy tree in all the entire Hundred-Acre Wood! My family tree!" Tigger was very excited.

Tigger climbed all over the tree, calling out for tiggers, but there was no answer. "I thought you were always there for me," he said despairingly.

Trudging through the snow, Roo found the giant tree and saw Tigger sitting in it. The friends hurried towards the tree, shouting for Tigger.

Tigger saw something moving towards him, calling out his name. "Looks like the whole family's finally here!" Tigger shouted excitedly.

He bounced down from the tree, and was surprised to see Pooh, Rabbit, Piglet, Eeyore, and Roo.

"What are you guys doing here? You're not tiggers!" Tigger said in frustration.

Just then a loud rumbling could be heard through the snow. A huge avalanche began to build up, rushing towards them. The others were afraid.

Tigger took control. "No time for dawdling, not a second to waste." And he bounced them all up into the tree.

But the avalanche rolled over Tigger.

"Tigger!" shouted the others in fear. They saw Tigger on a huge rock, going down with the avalanche. The avalanche was heading down the hill and over the cliff.

Roo had an idea. He wound himself up for the Whoop-de-Dooper Loop-de-Looper Alley-Ooper Bounce.

He bounced off the tree branches, and landed on Tigger's rock where Tigger was too exhausted to move.

But as the rock rolled off the cliff, Tigger and Roo wound themselves into position and bounced their way back to safety in the tree.

The storm gradually eased, and the friends realized that they had survived.

Tigger was very proud of Roo. "Why, that bounce was just as good as any old tigger . . ." But Tigger stopped himself, for he'd remembered that there weren't any other tiggers around.

Just then Owl and Kanga found them, followed by Christopher Robin.

"We were looking for Tigger looking for Tigger's family," Pooh explained.

The others recited Tigger's letter to him. Tigger was amazed. "You mean . . . you fellows are my family?" The others nodded.

"I should have seen it all along!" exclaimed Tigger happily.

The next day was Tigger's first family reunion, and he wanted to give everybody a present. Eeyore received Tigger's family room as his new home. Pooh received a honeypot. Piglet was happy to get a wheelbarrow full of firewood. Tigger promised not to bounce into Rabbit. And Roo received Tigger's gold locket.

"Wait half a minute! We still need a family portrait to put in it!" Tigger realized.

But Christopher Robin had already pulled out his camera. "Smile!" he ordered.

And everyone gathered close together and smiled.